Bank Financial Group

Ed Clark
President and CEO
TD Bank Financial Group

Dear Readers,

TD would like to present you with this gift to take home, read and enjoy!

Omar On Ice is a ... treasure that I hope you all wil... ...ove as much ... story, Omar discovers that ev... ...ne has their ... ...nts and that people are go... ...different th...

E... ...D is ... Grade One stu... ...

...el...

... year ... library

Ha... ...eading.

Ed Clark

For Thomas Kovalski

First published in English in a hardcover edition in 1999 by
Fitzhenry & Whiteside Limited, 195 Allstate Parkway, Markham, Ontario L3R 4T8

www.fitzhenry.ca godwit@fitzhenry.ca

This edition is based on the second edition (paperback) published in 2002
by Fitzhenry & Whiteside Limited.

Special edition prepared for the TD Grade One Book Giveaway Program.

Printed in Canada by Friesens Corporation

10 9 8 7 6 5 4 3 2 1

Also available in French: Quentin et le patin

ISBN 0-929095-19-7 (English) paperback
ISBN 0-929095-21-9 (French) paperback

Library and Archives Canada Cataloguing in Publication

Kovalski, Maryann
Omar on ice / Maryann Kovalski. — Special ed. prepared for the
TD Grade One Book Giveaway Program

Issued also in French under title: Quentin et le patin.
ISBN 0-929095-19-7

I. Canadian Children's Book Centre II. Title.

PS8571.O96O52 2004 jC813'.54 C2004-903489-8

Omar On Ice

Maryann Kovalski

The Canadian Children's Book Centre

Omar loved pictures.

1624

When he grew up, he was going
to be an artist. People would come
from all over to have him paint their
portraits. Maybe they would pay him
with candy. Omar liked red ju-jubes best.

Omar could not wait for school tomorrow.
Maybe Ms. Fudge would hold up
his picture in front of the class.

When
I
Grow up

When Ms. Fudge passed out the paper and pencils,
Omar felt the paper's smooth surface.
He loved the bright yellow of the pencil.

"I'm going to draw my rock collection," said Thomas.
"I'm making a rocket," said Bart.

"I will make a daisy," said Elsie.
Elsie drew every kind of flower.
She made it look so easy.

Soon the whole class was quietly
working away. Only Omar sat staring at his paper.

"What's wrong, Omar?"
asked Ms. Fudge.
"I can't think of anything
to draw," he said.
"Why don't you try
drawing something you love?"
suggested Ms. Fudge.

This gave Omar an idea.
He picked up his pencil
and started to draw.

"Ms. Fudge is going to
love this," he thought.

"What lovely rocks,
Thomas,"
said Ms. Fudge.
"Thank you," said Thomas.

When Ms. Fudge saw
Omar's drawing,
she was delighted.

"Why, Omar, this
picture is wonderful!"
Omar beamed.

"Look, class," said Ms. Fudge. "Hasn't Omar drawn a beautiful rock?"

"That's not a rock," said Omar. "That's my mother." Ms. Fudge looked again. She turned the drawing this way and that. "Yes, I see her now. Lovely." But Omar was not happy.

Ms. Fudge moved down the row and held up everyone's pictures, one by one.

"I'm a bad artist," growled Omar.

"Maybe it's your paper," said Elsie.

"Maybe you need another kind of pencil," said Thomas.

"It's not my pencil. It's me," said Omar.

Omar threw his drawing away.
"I'm just a bad artist," he said.

The bell rang for recess.

The whole class hurried outside.

Everyone laced up their skates and got on the ice—even Ms. Fudge. Everyone, except Omar.

"Why aren't you skating, Omar?" asked Thomas.
"You're the best skater in the whole class."
"I don't care if I'm the best skater. I want
to be the best artist," said Omar.

Elsie skated by. She did not
skate as well as
she drew flowers.
She fell down hard
on the ice. Omar
went to help her up.

"Rats," she said,
"I can't skate."
"Maybe your skates are
too big," said Omar.
"It's not my skates.
It's me. I'm just a bad skater."

"You're trying too hard," said Omar. "The thing about skating is to have fun. It's easy when you don't worry. Watch."

Omar took off slowly,
gliding like a bird in the sky.

Then he skated backwards like a sailboat
against the wind.

When he picked up speed,
he zoomed like a fast car.

Omar skated this way and that.
He whirled and swirled
from one end of the pond
to the other.

Soon Omar forgot all about being a bad artist.
He was having too much fun being a great skater.

When he jumped high in the air,
the whole class cheered.

"Look at Omar," said Thomas.
"Look at the ice," said Elsie.

On the ice were beautiful lines
wherever Omar had skated.

Elsie saw a turtle.
Thomas saw a bird.
Ms. Fudge was sure she saw Omar's
mother smiling.

It was true. Omar had drawn
many beautiful pictures on the ice.
Even he could see how good his drawings were.

"I was right," said Thomas,
as they made their way home.
"You just needed a different
kind of pencil."

Dear Reader: Here are some other great Canadian children's books.
The ones with a star (★) are suitable for readers aged 4 to 7.

2003 Award-winning Canadian Children's Books

ALBERTA CHILDREN'S BOOK OF THE YEAR AWARD
Troon Harrison. *Courage to Fly*. Illustrated by Zhong-Yang Huang. Calgary: Red Deer Press, 2002.

THE AMELIA FRANCES HOWARD-GIBBON ILLUSTRATOR'S AWARD
★ (Illustration) Pascal Milelli. *The Art Room* by Susan Vande Griek. Toronto: Groundwood Books/Douglas & McIntyre, 2002.

THE ANN CONNOR BRIMER AWARD
Lesley Choyce. *Shoulder the Sky*. Toronto: Dundurn Press, 2002.

ARTHUR ELLIS BEST JUVENILE CRIME AWARD
Norah McClintock. *Break and Enter*. Markham: Scholastic Canada, 2002.

BLUE SPRUCE AWARD
★ Matthew Napier. *Z is for Zamboni*. Illustrated by Melanie Rose. Chelsea, MI: Sleeping Bear Press, 2002.

CANADIAN AUTHORS ASSOCIATION BIRKS FAMILY FOUNDATION AWARD FOR BIOGRAPHY
Janet Lunn. *Maud's House of Dreams*. Toronto: Doubleday Canada, 2002.

CANADIAN LIBRARY ASSOCIATION BOOK OF THE YEAR FOR CHILDREN AWARD
Karen Levine. *Hana's Suitcase*. Toronto: Second Story Press, 2002.

CANADIAN LIBRARY ASSOCIATION YOUNG ADULT CANADIAN BOOK AWARD
Martha Brooks. *True Confessions of a Heartless Girl*. Toronto: Groundwood Books, 2002.

CHOCOLATE LILY YOUNG READERS' CHOICE AWARD
★ (Picture Book) Ainslie Manson. *Ballerinas Don't Wear Glasses.* Illustrated by Dean Griffiths. Victoria: Orca Book Publishers, 2000.
(Chapter Book/Novel) Irene N. Watts. *Remember Me*. Toronto: Tundra Books, 2000.

CHRISTIE HARRIS ILLUSTRATED CHILDREN'S LITERATURE PRIZE
★ Annette LeBox. *Salmon Creek*. Illustrated by Karen Reczuch. Toronto: Groundwood Books, 2002.

DIAMOND WILLOW AWARD
Arthur Slade. *Return of the Grudstone Ghosts.* Regina: Coteau Books, 2002.

ELIZABETH MRAZIK-CLEAVER CANADIAN PICTURE BOOK AWARD
★ (Illustration) Pierre Pratt. *Where's Pup?* by Dayle Ann Dodds. Toronto: Tundra Books, 2003.

THE GEOFFREY BILSON AWARD FOR HISTORICAL FICTION FOR YOUNG PEOPLE
Joan Clark. *The Word for Home*. Toronto: Penguin Books Canada, 2002.

GOLDEN EAGLE CHILDREN'S CHOICE BOOK AWARD
Monica Hughes. *Stormwarning*. Toronto: HarperCollins Canada, 2001.

GOVERNOR GENERAL'S LITERARY AWARDS
★ (Illustration) Allen Sapp. *The Song Within My Heart* by David Bouchard. Vancouver: Raincoast Books, 2002.
(Text) Glen Huser. *Stitches*. Toronto: Groundwood Books, 2003.

HACKMATACK CHILDREN'S CHOICE AWARD
(Fiction) Deborah Ellis. *The Breadwinner.* Toronto: Groundwood Books, 2000.
★ (Non-Fiction) Linda Bailey. *Adventures with the Vikings.* Toronto: Kids Can Press, 2001.

INFORMATION BOOK AWARD
Karen Levine. *Hana's Suitcase.* Toronto: Second Story Press, 2002.

THE IODE BOOK AWARD, MUNICIPAL CHAPTER OF TORONTO
★ Aubrey Davis. *Bagels from Benny.* Illustrated by Dušan Petričić. Toronto: Kids Can Press, 2003.

MANITOBA YOUNG READERS' CHOICE AWARD
Virginia Frances Schwartz. *If I Just Had Two Wings.* Toronto: Stoddart Kids, 2001.

THE NATIONAL CHAPTER OF CANADA IODE VIOLET DOWNEY BOOK AWARD
Karen Levine. *Hana's Suitcase.* Toronto: Second Story Press, 2002.

NORMA FLECK AWARD FOR CANADIAN CHILDREN'S NON-FICTION
Larry Loyie with Constance Brissenden. *As Long as the Rivers Flow.* Illustrated by Heather D. Holmlund. Toronto: Groundwood Books, 2002.

OTTAWA BOOK AWARDS/ PRIX DE LIVRE D'OTTAWA
Brian Doyle. *Mary Ann Alice.* Toronto: Groundwood Books, 2003.

THE RED CEDAR BOOK AWARDS
(Fiction) Deborah Ellis. *The Breadwinner.* Toronto: Groundwood Books, 2000.
(Non-Fiction) Linda Bailey. *Adventures in the Middle Ages.* Illustrated by Bill Slavin. Toronto: Kids Can Press, 2000.

RED MAPLE AWARD
Gayle Friesen. *Losing Forever.* Toronto: Kids Can Press, 2002.

ROCKY MOUNTAIN BOOK AWARD
Deborah Ellis. *The Breadwinner.* Toronto: Groundwood Books, 2000.

RUTH SCHWARTZ CHILDREN'S BOOK AWARD
(Picture Book) Richard Thompson. *The Night Walker.* Illustrated by Martin Springett. Toronto: Fitzhenry & Whiteside, 2002.
(YA-Middle Reader) Deborah Ellis. *Parvana's Journey.* Toronto: Groundwood Books, 2002.

SASKATCHEWAN BOOK AWARDS
Judith Silverthorne. *Dinosaur Hideout.* Regina: Coteau Books, 2003.

SHEILA A. EGOFF CHILDREN'S BOOK PRIZE
James Heneghan. *Flood.* Toronto: Groundwood Books, 2002.

SHINING WILLOW AWARD
★ Hazel Hutchins. *TJ and the Cats.* Victoria: Orca Book Publishers, 2002.

THE SILVER BIRCH AWARD
(Fiction) Eric Walters. *Camp X.* Toronto: Penguin Books Canada, 2002.
(Non-Fiction) Karen Levine. *Hana's Suitcase.* Toronto: Second Story Press, 2002.

SNOW WILLOW AWARD
Cathy Beveridge. *Offside.* Saskatoon: Thistledown Press, 2001.

TORGI LITERARY AWARDS
★ (Print Braille) Robin Muller. *Badger's New House.* Toronto: Scholastic Canada/North Winds, 2002.
(Audio) Karen Levine. *Hana's Suitcase.* Toronto: Second Story Press, 2002.

WHITE PINE AWARD
Gillian Chan. *A Foreign Field.* Toronto: Kids Can Press, 2002.

WINTERSET AWARD
Joan Clark. *The Word for Home.* Toronto: Penguin Books Canada, 2002.

YOUNG READER'S CHOICE AWARD
(Intermediate) Gordon Korman. *No More Dead Dogs.* New York: Hyperion Books, 2000.

TD Canadian Children's Book Week

Over 500,000 Grade One children across Canada will receive
a copy of this book, *Omar On Ice*. This special book giveaway is part
of the celebration of TD Canadian Children's Book Week
which takes place from October 30 to November 6, 2004.

During TD Canadian Children's Book Week, which is the largest annual
festival of reading and Canadian children's literature, Canadian authors,
illustrators, and storytellers tour across the country, visiting schools and libraries,
talking about their books and meeting young readers.

Book Week also inspires many more activities and local events celebrating
Canadian children's books and their creators.

The Grade One Book Giveaway and TD Canadian Children's Book Week
are organized by the Canadian Children's Book Centre.
The Canadian Children's Book Centre is a national non-profit organization,
founded in 1976, dedicated to promoting the reading, writing, and illustrating
of Canadian books for young readers.

TD Canadian Children's Book Week is made possible through the generous
support of the following sponsors and funders:

Title Sponsor: TD Bank Financial Group
Major Sponsor: The Canada Council for the Arts
Associate Sponsors: Imperial Oil Foundation, Penguin Group (Canada),
Toronto Public Library, Library and Archives Canada,
Ontario Arts Council, Amazon.ca.

For more information about the Canadian Children's Book Centre,
and about TD Canadian Children's Book Week, please visit our websites:
www.bookcentre.ca and **www.bookweek.ca.**
You can also call us, or write to us at:

The Canadian Children's Book Centre
40 Orchard View Blvd., Suite 101
Toronto, Ontario M4R 1B9

Telephone: (416) 975-0010
Fax: (416) 975-8970
Email: info@bookcentre.ca
Websites: www.bookcentre.ca
www.bookweek.ca

The Canadian Children's Book Centre

Bringing Canadian books and young readers together.